Beyond the Rolling River

"I say, old thing, you are rather wet, aren't you?" remarked the tall, blue man after he had fished Toby out of the water in a large fishing net. "I was fishing for Glimrod, the great Tuning Fork. It's so important it doesn't fall into the wrong hands. Whoever holds it in his hand controls the weather, and whoever controls the weather rules the world." Slubblejum, the nethercat, who had been resting on a nearby ledge, sat up and listened more carefully. To rule the world!

Also available in Lions

The Haunting of Cassie Palmer *Vivien Alcock*
The Prism Tree *Kate Andrew*
Just Like Jenny *Sandy Asher*
The Making of Fingers Finnigan *Berlie Doherty*
The Long Secret *Louise Fitzhugh*
Private, Keep Out! *Gwen Grant*
Just Ask for Diamond *Anthony Horowitz*
I'll Go My Own Way *Mollie Hunter*
Chain of Fire *Beverley Naidoo*
The Silver Crown *Robert O'Brien*
Charley *Joan Robinson*
Double the Boys *Finola Sumner*
Double Vision *Gilli Wright*

Kate Andrew

Beyond the Rolling River

Illustrated by Chris Riddell

Lions

First published in Great Britain by
HarperCollins Publishers Ltd 1988
First published in Lions 1991

Lions is an imprint of
the Children's Division, part of
HarperCollins Publishers Ltd,
77–85 Fulham Palace Road, London W6 8JB

Printed and bound in Great Britain by
HarperCollins Book Manufacturing, Glasgow

To Kevin and Stephen,
to make things even

The Storm

Toby was on his way to the river to look for dragonflies. He had been staying on his uncle's farm for the summer holidays, and had just discovered that collecting insects was much more interesting than looking at sheep or cows. So this fine, hot Monday afternoon he had set off straight after lunch, armed with a plastic box and an old tea strainer that his aunt had lent him to use as an insect net.

He had not gone very far when he realised that he was in for a storm, or rather, out for a storm, which was worse. He turned to go back home, but he had left it too late. The air was split by a sudden flash of lightning, and at almost the same moment there was a tremendous roar of thunder and the rain began. Toby started to run as fast as his legs would carry him, but in two minutes he was soaked to the skin, and so blinded by the rain and the flashes of lightning that he couldn't see where he was going. It was like running through a waterfall. He didn't see the old tree root on the river bank, tripped over it and felt something give him a bang on the head. Then all he knew was that he was falling down and down through the roaring water...

He woke to find himself lying on a kind of mossy bank, which felt so soft and comfortable that he didn't want to move at first. He stretched lazily, then noticed that he was surrounded by water.

That's funny, he thought. I must have fallen in the river – I wonder why I haven't drowned. Or perhaps I *have* drowned, and now I'm just a ghost. He found this rather exciting, and thought of going and haunting his friends at school. But after he had given himself a poke or two, he decided that he wasn't a ghost after all, but that something must have happened to his lungs, so that he could now breathe like a fish.

"Perhaps it was something to do with that storm," he said out loud.

"Very odd storm indeed," agreed a small voice, apparently coming from a nearby rock. Toby stood up and looked all round, but he

couldn't see anyone.

"I'm glad you have revived anyway," said the rock again. "I was beginning to think you had knocked yourself out for good." Toby looked more closely, and could just make out a small creature, something like a lizard with a ridge on its back, almost exactly the same colour as the rock it was sitting on.

"It's rude to stare," said the creature firmly. "Have you never seen a chameleon before? I'm Hardly Visible."

"Yes, I can see that," said Toby.

"But you may call me Hardly," it added. "And what's *your* name?"

"Oh, I see what you mean. I'm Toby Jones."

"What does it mean?" asked Hardly Visible.

"It doesn't mean anything. It's just my name," said Toby.

"Of course it means something," said Hardly. "What do you want to be when you grow up?"

"An entomologist," said Toby. (He had just decided that yesterday.)

"Then it means small-boy-with-sandy-hair-and-blue-eyes-who-wants-to-be-an-entomologist," stated the chameleon. "By the way, what's an entomologist?"

"It's someone who is keen on insects," said Toby.

"Mmmm, nice!" said Hardly. "Do you prefer them roasted or raw?"

"No, I don't *eat* them," said Toby. "I just study their behaviour and all that. That's why I have this . . ." He broke off and looked round for the plastic box, but it seemed to have got lost in the storm. He felt in his pocket for the tea strainer, and took it out to make sure it was all right.

"What's that?" asked the chameleon.

"It's really a tea strainer," said Toby, "but I'm using it for catching insects until I get a real insect net."

At this, the chameleon suddenly recited,

"A gipsy called Rosie O'Lee
Would read fortunes in tea leaves for free;
She said, 'Heavens above,
It's not tea leaves I love,
It's the gin that I put in the tea!'"

"Well!" exclaimed Toby. "Fancy a chameleon reciting poetry!"

"Oh, that's nothing," replied Hardly. "I had an aunt once who used to recite Latin odes. Till she got eaten by a rattlesnake. And that was no Latin matter, I tell you!" He bounced up and down at his own joke, then went on, "Odd about you not eating insects. But everything seems a bit odd today. Like that storm just now. Washed me into the river, then washed you in on top of me, and then stopped all of a sudden as if somebody had switched it off in the middle."

"So you are lost as well?" asked Toby.

"Not lost, exactly," said Hardly Visible. "It's just that I prefer to live on the banks of the Catanooga River, rather than at the bottom of the water."

"The *what*, did you say?" asked Toby. "This is the River Werrin, isn't it?"

"Not at all, old son," said the chameleon cheerfully, looking up at the boy, who was about a hundred times bigger than himself. "It's been called the Catanooga as long as I have known it, and I've lived here all my life. I'm nearly eighteen, you know."

"You're nearly eighteen years old?" asked Toby in astonishment.

"*Weeks*, silly!" said the chameleon.

"Well, whatever you call the river, we'd better find a way out of it," said Toby. "The sides are very steep here, but they may be better lower down. Are you coming?"

By way of reply, the chameleon gave a jump onto the boy's shoulder, and they set off downstream. The river bed was pebbly, with a few large rocks here and there. A few fishes were going about their own business, and everything was quiet and peaceful and pale green and wavy. Toby was really beginning to enjoy his under-water walk when suddenly, as he turned a bend in the river, he nearly tripped over the tail of a large, scaly crocodile.

2   Slubblejum and Friends

Hardly Visible gave a screech, and dived into Toby's pocket. Toby did not screech, but dived just as quickly behind a nearby rock. Fortunately for them, the crocodile was looking the other way, and did not notice them. It was too busy watching something else coming through the water towards it. Toby heaved a sigh of relief, and cautiously looked out from behind the rock.

He thought for a moment that the other animal was a very large otter, then as it swam up and stopped by the crocodile, he saw that it was in fact a cat. At least, it was a kind of a cat. It certainly had a cat's face and cat's eyes, and a kind of whiskers, but its feet were webbed, and instead of having fur, it was covered all over in greeny-blue scales, like a tropical fish. Also, it was much bigger than a normal cat, and was more than a match for the fat crocodile. Toby was so astonished that he forgot to be scared, and gazed at the scene with his mouth open, until he swallowed too much water for comfort, and shut it again.

"Ug, you *bad* crocodile!" said the strange cat. He spoke with a strong cattish accent, so that every word sounded half like a miaow. "I've been looking for you everywhere. Now we've wasted half the day, and you know what they say about early worms, don't you? An early worm has a silver lining. Or was it the early worm that has no turning? Anyway, you have to be scrubbed."

The crocodile waggled its long tail, and looked rather sheepish, if crocodiles can look sheepish. Toby saw that the "cat" was carrying something in its front paws, which turned out to be a bottle of shampoo and a large scrubbing brush. He started pouring the shampoo over the croc's back, and scrubbing it vigorously, talking to it as he went along.

"How can I get you ready if you run off like that? Don't you know it's the Croc of the Year Show tomorrow, and Mrs Betaslink will have my cat-guts for garters if we are not ready. Not that I care what she says, really, but a stitch in time

saves two in the bush, you know." He started singing to himself as he worked,

> *"'Crocodile, crocodile, where have you been?'*
> *'I've been up the river to visit a queen —*
> *The queen was delightful, all sunburnt*
>   *and brown,*
> *But I got indigestion from eating her crown.'"*

By this time the crocodile was getting rather fidgety, and it turned round the other way. The "cat" turned with it, so they both saw Toby at the same time. Hardly Visible made himself Wholly Invisible, and Toby flattened himself behind the rock and tried to look as much like a piece of moss as possible, but it was no use. The scaly cat came over to investigate.

"Well, I do declare!" he cried. "It's a yee-uman, and a jee-unior yee-uman at that! *So* glad you dropped in — you're just in time for tea, and Ug is getting rather hungry, aren't you, old croc?" He patted the crocodile on the head and roared with laughter at his own joke. Then, seeing that Toby was trying to slip away quietly, he gave a sudden pounce and blocked his path.

"Not so fast, young yee-uman, we haven't been introduced. What's your name?"

"Toby Jones," said the boy, feeling rather

like the meat in the sandwich between the cat and the crocodile.

"And I," announced the scaly cat, "am Slubblejum Orestes Snatchington. But you may call me Sir. And this, as you may have gathered, is Ug." He waved a paw at the crocodile, which was now sitting on its haunches and snapping idly at the passing fish.

"Is that short for Ugly?" asked Toby. The crocodile snarled.

"Short for nothing!" said Slubblejum. "What's wrong with Ug anyway? A nose by any other name would smell a treat, you know. Actually, he belongs to my neighbour, Mrs Betaslink, but she lets me look after him on special occasions. Usually when there is work to be done," he added gloomily. Then suddenly, he brightened up and gave a wide, whiskery grin.

"I know!" he said. "Why don't *you* finish scrubbing Ug, and *I'll* supervise." He saw the look on Toby's face and added, "You're not frightened, are you? Remember – he who fights and runs away makes Jack a dull boy."

Toby thought about this for a moment, then decided to try a bit of flattery.

"I'm afraid I wouldn't be half as good at the job as you are, Sir," he said. "After all, cats are experts at washing, aren't they?"

The last thing he expected was the reaction he got to this remark. Slubblejum suddenly leaped about three feet above the riverbed, uttering the most dreadful "Wrrrreéeeooooouuuu!" imaginable. Toby was so startled he jumped behind the rock again.

"Oh, my scales and whiskers!" exclaimed Slubblejum when he came to earth again. "*Cat*, he called me! *Cat*, he said! Oh, my tail and toenails!"

"Well please, Sir," said Toby, who had no idea what he had said wrong, "If you're not a c . . . I mean, what are you then?"

Before Slubblejum could answer, they were interrupted by a great splash and flurry, as another scaly "cat" arrived on the scene. The newcomer had bright orange scales and a bow of blue ribbon round her neck.

"Oh, there you are, Mrs Betaslink," said Slubblejum with a rather nervous grin. "I've nearly finished scrubbing Ug."

Mrs Betaslink was out of breath, and obviously not in the best of tempers.

"About time too!" she said. "What have you been doing all this time, I'd like to know? Playing games, I suppose, instead of getting on with the job. Well, you'd better not play any games tomorrow, young whisker-snapper! We have to set off for the Show at ten o'clock sharp, and I want his teeth cleaned and his scales oiled before that."

"Don't cross your bridges before they are hatched," said Slubblejum. Mrs Betaslink shook her paw at him.

"And don't try getting clever with me," she said. "I know you. You're a great lover of crocodiles when it comes to strolling around the riverbed and playing ball all day, but it's a different matter when there is work to be done. Well, let me tell you . . ."

Slubblejum had had enough of this. "Wreou!" he interrupted, pointing at Toby. "It's all his fault. He kept me talking."

What cheek! thought Toby.

"*And* he called me a cat, so he did! Imagine comparing a handsome nethercat with an insignificant, land-lubbing mouse-eater!"

"A *what*?" gasped Toby. Mrs Betaslink came across and started poking him with her paw.

"That's quite enough from you, young man," she said. "You just learn to treat your elders and betters with respect, that's what!"

"I beg your pardon," said Toby politely, "but you see, I've never actually met a *nether*cat before."

"Never met a nether..."

"Well, I never!"

exclaimed Slubblejum and Mrs Betaslink both at once. Then, quite forgetting their quarrel, they began to sing a song together, while doing a dance around the crocodile at the same time. It went like this:

"The nethercats are elegant,
So slippery and sleek,
And some live on the riverbed
And some live in the creek;
Their shiny tails are wrapped in scales,
They swim just like a fish —
Oh, you'll never catch a nethercat,
No matter how you wish!

No other kind of animal
Can possibly compare
With a slim and slimy nethercat
With scales instead of hair;
There's cats of fur who love to purr,
There's valuable mink,
But they'll never match a nethercat.
No matter what they think!"

While the nethercats were singing, Toby took the opportunity to slip away unnoticed. As their voices faded in the distance, once more everything was quiet but for the gentle swishing of the stream.

"There's a nice pair for you!" said a small voice near his left ear.

"Whoops!" said Toby, for he had neither heard nor felt Hardly Visible climbing onto his shoulder. "You made me jump."

"Never trust a nethercat, no matter what you do," chanted Hardly, imitating the nethercats' song.

"I must say, I thought at first he was going to pounce on me as if I were a mouse," said Toby. "Slubblejum, I mean."

"*You* felt like a mouse! What do you think *I* felt like?" exclaimed the chameleon, and he went on,

> *"There once was a mouse (not a vole),*
> *Who sang hymns all day long down his*
> * hole;*
> *When asked to explain*
> *He said, 'Why it's plain —*
> *Mice singing is good for mice soul!'"*

Then he started jumping up and down on Toby's shoulder, slapping his hardly visible side with a hardly visible paw, and saying, "He, he! Mice singing is good for mice soul, get it?"

Toby was just starting to say, "I've got it, but I'm not sure that I want it," when there was a sudden Swoosh! and he found himself being hauled out of the river inside a very large fishing net on the end of a stout pole.

3 The Lightning Conductor

"Phew, that was a heavy one!" said a voice a long way above Toby's head. Then, getting a bit closer, it added, "Sorry, old bean, thought you were a fish, what!"

Toby struggled out of the net, shook the water off himself like a dog, and found himself gazing up at a very unusual person. Everything about him was long and pointed. He had long, pointed fingers and long, pointed toes; long, pointed elbows and a long, pointed nose. He was dressed in a grey top hat, morning coat and striped trousers, and had a red carnation in his buttonhole. In fact, he looked more as if he were on his way to a wedding than a day's fishing. But that was not what made Toby gasp in astonishment. The general effect of an old-fashioned English gentleman was spoiled by just one thing. His skin was a rather pleasant and delicate shade

of blue.

"I say, old thing, you are rather wet, aren't you?" he remarked. He had twinkling blue eyes, and seemed quite amused at the sight of Toby. He sat down on the grass, making himself a bit nearer the boy's level, and crossed his long legs comfortably. "Never mind, you'll soon dry off in this sunshine, what!"

24

In fact, the sun was now blazing down on them with an almost tropical heat. Toby stopped staring at the fisherman for a moment and looked around him. They were in a large meadow full of buttercups, and in the distance he could see a range of snow-capped mountains. It was certainly not a part of the countryside he had ever seen before.

"I was fishing for Glimrod," the blue gentleman was saying. "Slipped out of my hand during the storm. Dashed careless of me, I must admit." Before Toby could ask who or what Glimrod was, he went on, "It's the Great Tuning Fork. You know what a tuning fork is, don't you?"

Toby was not too sure.

"It's a kind of metal stick with two prongs, and it keeps the orchestra in tune. Well, Glimrod is the same kind of shape, but it keeps the weather in tune. Symphony of the elements and all that, you know. It's the

Thunder-shaking
Lightning-waking
Hail and rain and rainbow-making
Snowflake-flaking
Earthquake-quaking
Wondrous Tuning Fork."

"Really?" said Toby, as he couldn't think of

anything else to say.

"Oh, I should have explained – I'm the Lightning Conductor, you know. Real name's Zwrbdockshlimpquaftjengvyx, but don't let that worry you." He stuck out a long, blue hand for Toby to shake.

"I'm Toby Jones," said the boy for the third time since lunch.

"Tobijones – I like it," said the Lightning Conductor. "I'm a WORC, you know. Wise Old Rulers of the Cosmos," he explained, as Toby looked puzzled. "Of course, I'm only a junior member, in fact Earth is my first big assignment. And if I don't find Glimrod before the Council hear about it, I'm likely to be sent back to some boring old asteroid for the next five hundred years. Anyway, how do you like my outfit?" He brushed an imaginary speck of dust from his lapel. "I read somewhere about the blue-blooded Englishman, and I thought if I modelled myself on him I would pass unnoticed. When on Earth, do as the Earthians do and all that, what!"

"They're not usually *really* blue," explained Toby. "It's just the way people talk – I don't know why."

"Oh, is that so?" asked the Lightning Conductor in surprise. "Well, colour's not important anyway, old fruit. The real problem is

Glimrod, what!" And he went on explaining.

Now, while Toby and the Lightning Conductor were talking, neither of them had noticed that a scaly, cat-like figure had swum silently down the stream, and was now sitting on a narrow ledge just below the overhanging river bank. This happened to be Slubblejum's favourite spot, and just now he was having his usual daydream about what he would do when he got to be King Slubblejum the First. He had not been taking any notice of the two voices on the bank, but now he heard one of them say some words like "power" and "rule", which he found rather interesting, and he began to listen carefully.

"It's so important that it doesn't fall into the wrong hands," the Lightning Conductor was saying. "Harmony is what it is all about, but there are a lot of people who will see it in terms of power. After all, whoever holds it in his hands controls the weather, and whoever controls the weather rules the world."

At that Slubblejum really sat up and took notice. Not only to rule the nethercats, but to rule the world — just think of that!

"Things are going haywire already," went on the Lightning Conductor. "It's raining in the Sahara, the North Pole is having its first ever heatwave, and there is a tropical monsoon over

Greater Manchester. I mean, I know they are used to rain and all that, but this is ridiculous!"

"Can't you just use magic to find it?" asked Toby.

"Great Shooting Stars, I'm not magic! And neither is Glimrod. It's a finely-tuned scientific instrument, designed to respond to the sound of the human voice. Or similar species, of course."

Slubblejum wondered for a moment if he counted as a similar species, and decided that he did, at least as far as voice was concerned. He considered he had a very fine speaking voice – the sort of voice that launched a thousand ships, he mused. He brought his thoughts back to the conversation on the bank.

"You must admit it was magic that I could breathe like a fish when I fell in the river," Toby was saying.

"Shouldn't think so, old man," said the Lightning Conductor. "It's much more likely that

Glimrod's energy waves have hyper-oxygenated the water. I definitely heard a splash when it fell, and it is such a powerful instrument that even if it landed miles out to sea, the effect would still work its way up the river in no time at all. And that gives me a great idea — why don't you go and search the sea for it, while I carry on up the river?"

"Search the *what*?" exclaimed Toby.

"The sea, old bean. You know, that blue stuff that surrounds . . ."

"Yes, I know what the sea is," interrupted Toby. "But it is rather big, isn't it?"

The Lightning Conductor looked rather hurt.

"Well, we have to start somewhere, old chap," he said in a huffy tone of voice. "And if you can't give a bit of help when a fellow's in a tight corner, it's not very sporting, that's all I can say."

"I didn't say I wouldn't help," said Toby. "I

was just wondering where to begin, that's all."

"Jolly good show!" said the Lightning Conductor, cheering up at once. "I knew I could depend on you. Well, the only place to begin is here, of course. And from here you have to find the sea, so I suggest you follow the river downstream. It's sure to get to the sea sooner or later." He got to his feet and picked up his fishing net.

"And I suppose we'd better make a jolly old ronday-voo, what!" he added. "You see that hill over there?" Toby looked where the bony blue finger was pointing. "It's called Halfway Hill, because it stands halfway between the Catanooga River and the Nevareva Desert, and you can see it for miles around. When you've anything to report, just come back and light a bonfire on top of the hill, and I will be with you before you can say Alpha Andromeda. Good luck, Tobijones!"

"Okay," said Toby. "Cheerio, and see you soon!" And he set off to follow the river downstream.

"Cheerio, and see you soon!" echoed Slubblejum to himself. And he slipped back noiselessly into the water.

4   In Search of Glimrod

Toby was making his way along the river bank, knocking the heads off dandelion clocks and whistling, "Oh, I do like to be beside the seaside."

"Well, isn't this exciting!" squeaked a small voice near his left foot.

"Oh, Hardly!" he exclaimed. "I wondered where you had got to."

"Just catching a few water bugs, old fruit," said the chameleon, imitating the Lightning Conductor's voice. "After all, one does have to eat, doesn't one? Funny-looking feller, I must say. He reminds me of another blue-blooded gent:

> *"Lord Archibald Arlington-Grue*
> *Had blood of the vividest blue.*
> *When cut on the hand*
> *He cried, 'I can't stand*
> *That truly blue hue. Boo, hoo, hoo!'"*

"Did you hear what he was saying about the Great Glimrod?" asked Toby.

"Indubitably, old bean," said Hardly. "You are to search the world for it, and bring it to Halfway Hill by tomorrow at the latest. No problem at all! Anyway, as I'm not doing anything special this afternoon, I may as well come with you. To protect you from dangers by the wayside, and all that."

The idea of the chameleon protecting him from anything larger than an earwig struck Toby as rather funny, but he was glad to have some company, so the two friends set off resolutely towards the sea. And no doubt they would soon have found it, but for one thing. They were both, for different reasons, very fond of insects. So when a large, glittering, yellow dragonfly flew up from the river's edge and across a nearby field, neither the boy nor the chameleon could resist setting off in pursuit.

They chased it across that field, over the wall and across the next one, until at last they both stopped out of breath, and found that not only was there no dragonfly in sight, but no field either. They couldn't see the wall they had climbed; they couldn't see any trees or hedges; they couldn't see any grass. All they could see was miles and miles of sand, with here and there

a sand dune for variety.

"How did we manage to come so far in just five minutes?" exclaimed Toby. "We'd better turn round and go straight back to the river before we get lost." The chameleon agreed, and they retraced their steps carefully for five minutes. Then ten minutes. Then half-an-hour.

"We're lost," said Toby.

"We're lost," agreed Hardly.

"Oh well," said Toby, "I suppose we'd better keep moving. If we keep the sun on our left all the time, at least we won't be going round in circles."

The sand was difficult to walk on, so Hardly Visible hopped onto Toby's shoulder again. Toby didn't have anyone's shoulder to hop onto, so he just had to keep on walking. And the farther he walked, the more he seemed to be getting nowhere. Every bit of the desert looked exactly like the bit they had just left behind, except that when he turned round he could see his own footprints stretching away into the distance. The sun was getting hotter and hotter, and Toby was getting more and more thirsty, while even Hardly Visible stopped his usual chatter and just clung to the boy's shoulder in silence.

Then, far away on the horizon, Toby saw a small, dark speck. The small, dark speck grew into a large, dark speck, and the large, dark speck grew into something with legs, and the something with legs grew a head and a hump and a Superior Expression, and finally stopped in front of him and said,

"Hrrrmmmph!"

"A camel!" cried Toby. "What a stroke of luck!"

"Hrrrmmmph!" said the camel again. "It would be more accurate to ascribe our encounter to the intervention of fate, since according to the law of probability, the chances of meeting another living being in a desert of this size in the course of one day's journey are approximately nine hundred and ninety-eight thousand, six hundred and forty-five against. In other words," it concluded, "I'm pleased to meet you."

"You can say that again!" said Toby, then hastily introduced himself, in case the camel took him at his word.

"Charmed, I'm sure," said the camel. "I am Camellia Camelus Dromedarius. But you may call be Camellia," she added with an air of gracious condescension.

"And this," said Toby, "is Hardly Visible."

"Well, don't worry about it," said Camellia. "It's probably a mirage."

"No, I mean this is my chameleon friend, and he is called Hardly Visible," said Toby. He stretched out his hand and the chameleon jumped onto it.

"Hrrrmmmph!" said the camel, and gave a loud sniff.

"Please could you help us?" asked Toby. "We have to get back to the Catanooga River because that's the quickest way to find the sea and the Lightning Conductor has lost his tuning fork and the weather is going all haywire and we have to find it and bring it back to Halfway Hill and we're both very thirsty and..."

"That's enough!" interrupted Camellia. "Simultaneity is not conducive to the attainment of diversified objectives. In other words, one thing at a time!" She knelt down on the sand.

"Circumstances indicate a more expeditious locomotion," she said. "In other words, get on my back. I don't know about *that*," she added, looking down her nose at the chameleon.

"Members of the species Camelus Dromedarius are characterised by a supercilious demeanour," remarked Hardly Visible. "In other words, snobby." With that, he hopped onto the camel's back, followed by Toby, who settled himself as comfortably as possible as Camellia got to her feet.

"Do you like my camel-hair coat?" asked Hardly brightly. Camellia set off with an ambling, shambling rhythm that made Toby feel slightly seasick at first. He noticed that the sky was getting very hazy, but thought that perhaps a heat haze was normal in the desert. However, by the time they had got over the next sand dune, the haze had turned into an unmistakeable pea-soup fog.

"Brrrr!" said Camellia. "Climatic conditions are manifesting an unprecedented degree of humidity. In other words, it's wet! What was that you were saying about toasting forks and a Thunderbolt Detector?"

"Tuning fork," said Toby, "and the Lightning Conductor." And he told her all about it.

"Hrrrmmmph!" said Camellia when he had finished. Then she started muttering to herself, "Hmmm, tuning fork... I wonder... No, there couldn't possibly be any connection... And yet..."

"Camellia, what are you grunting about?" asked Toby.

"It's probably not important," said Camellia, "but your story reminded me about an odd couple who live somewhere along the seashore.

I'll tell you about them:

> "There once was a musical musing man
> Who dwelt by the dreaming sea;
> He ate his fish with a tuning fork
> And never a word said he,
> He ate his fish
> In a silvery dish
> With cinnamon spice
> To make it nice —
> Oh, he ate his fish with a tuning fork,
> And never a word said he.
>
> He had a wife who was dear as life
> And never a word said she,
> While he went to wait for a plaice or
> skate
> By the gleaming, dreaming sea.
> She cooked his fish
> In a silvery dish
> With cinnamon spice
> To make it nice,
> And she ate her fish with a tuning fork,
> And never a word said she.
>
> The years went by and they seemed to fly
> As happy as life can be,
> For as neither ever did speak a word
> They never could disagree.
> They lived in bliss

With a fish in a dish,
And cinnamon spice
To make it nice,
And he ate his fish with a tuning fork,
and never a word said he (or she),

Oh, they ate their fish with a tuning fork,
And dreamt of the dreaming sea."

"That's great!" said Toby when Camellia had finished. "And do you know where this strange couple live? They may have heard something about Glimrod, or at least they may help us to look for it, if they are interested in tuning forks."

"It was someone from Fiddlington-on-Sea who taught me the poem," said Camellia, "so probably they live there."

"Fiddlington-on-Sea, here we come!" said Toby. "If only we can get out of this silly fog."

But the silly fog just went on and on, in fact it seemed to be even worse than before, and Toby could hardly see the camel's head in front of him. Suddenly Camellia stopped dead as she nearly bumped into something. It was a palm tree.

"Well!" she exclaimed. "Our circumambulations have terminated in an alternative source of refreshment. In other words, we've found an oasis." While they were groping their way

towards the pool, the fog decided to clear away and they could see the sun again. It was now low on the horizon, and they decided to stay there for the night, and set off to find the river again next morning.

There were dates growing in the palm trees, and after they had all had a long, refreshing drink from the pool, Toby went climbing to throw some down. He thought he had never tasted anything so delicious as that date supper, while they sat and watched the desert sun setting behind the palm trees, and the millions of stars coming out in the deep, dark sky. Then Toby settled down in the shelter of the camel, and Hardly Visible settled down in the shelter of Toby, and very soon they were all fast asleep.

5   Desert Dreams

Toby was woken early in the morning by the sound of something splashing, and for a few moments he couldn't think where he was. He thought he was on a boat with an outboard motor going, and then he realised that the water was the pool of the oasis, and the "motor" was Camellia, who was still peacefully snoring.

There seemed to be a log floating in the pool, and he watched it lazily, and wondered how it could have got there. He was sure it had not been there last night. It was quite a large log, mossy green, and rather rough-looking, and it seemed to be drifting round the pool in a large circle. It had two knobs on top, towards the front end, with a flat piece of log sticking out in front of the knobs, and a longer piece of log following behind. As it came round the near side of the pool for the second time, one of the "knobs" suddenly opened, showing a large, green eye, and winked at him.

Toby was so startled that he jumped straight onto Camellia's back, shouting "Crocodile!" at the top of his voice. The camel woke with a start, shaking her head, and blowing through her lips with a great, noisy "Prrrmmmph!" as she got to her feet.

The crocodile started hauling itself out of the pool, grinning at them in a friendly fashion. Toby, of course, was getting quite used to crocodiles by now, but Camellia certainly wasn't. She at once started charging across the desert as if a horde of demons were after her. The crocodile set off in pursuit, but its short legs were not really designed for speed on the sand, and it soon gave up the chase. Camellia galloped on in a panic.

In between trying not to fall off, Toby twisted round to see what was going on behind them. He saw a shiny, cat-like figure leap out of the pool, overtake the crocodile and fall into a furious temper with it, hitting it on the head with its fists, which probably hurt itself more than the crocodile. Then it climbed onto the crocodile's back, and the pair of them waddled off in the other direction.

"Whoa, whoa, Camellia!" shouted Toby. "It's

gone now. It's all right, there's no need to panic."

"Hrrrmmmph!" said Camellia, slowing down and putting on a superior air. "I was merely demonstrating the benefits of swift evasive action in an emergency, that's all. In other words, run for it."

Toby told her what had happened behind them, and asked, "What do you make of that?"

"I must acknowledge the unprofitability of speculation," said Camellia. "In other words, I don't know."

"It's just as well I had slipped into your pocket to keep warm during the night," piped up Hardly Visible, as he clambered out. "Just think – I might have been stranded at that oasis for ever, and have had to live on cold water and palm tree bugs for the rest of my life."

"Are there such things as palm tree bugs?" asked Toby with interest.

"Of course there are," said Hardly. "What do you think I had for supper?" And then he added, "Talking of food,

"There was a young lady called Nelly,
Who ate a large portion of jelly,
When she rode on a horse
The jelly, of course,
All joggled around in her . . ."

"Hrrrmmmph!" said Camellia rather loudly. "I think we had better take our bearings again. Now let's see. The elevation of the sun above the horizon in conjunction with the magnetic vibrations in my left front hoof, indicate a bearing of two degrees north of south-south-west, which should bring us to the Catanooga River in thirty-five and a half minutes. Approximately." She set off plodding again.

Toby had by now quite got over his seasickness, or rather, his camel-sickness, and was finding Camellia's ambling walk rather soothing. As they went on, his thoughts somehow fell into rhythm with her steps, and he found he was making up a poem in his head. That's odd! he thought. I don't usually write poetry, but I seem to be doing a lot of unusual things these days. He recited his poem out loud:

> *"I wish I were a camel with a hump*
> *upon my back,*
> *An admirable animal that roams the*
> *desert track;*
> *The lord of all I saw from the Sahara to*
> *the Nile,*
> *I'd view the world around me with a*
> *supercilious smile."*

"That's all very well," said Camellia, "but the desert can get boring, you know. There are times when I would much rather be an elephant." Then the poem turned into a kind of game, with each of them thinking of odder and odder things they would like to be. The result went like this:

Camellia:
> *"I wish I were an elephant elumphing*
> *through the trees,*
> *I'd have a tail at either end and wave*
> *them in the breeze;*
> *I'd go magniphalentiously upon my*
> *mighty way,*
> *And make my voice resound from*
> *Bangalore to Mandalay."*

Toby:

>*"I wish I were a panda in the forests of*
>   *Manchu,*
>*Awaking from my winter sleep to chew*
>   *the new bamboo,*
>*For nothing in all China's lands could*
>   *possibly be grander*
>*Than a jolly roly-poly furry purry patchy*
>   *panda."*

Camellia:

>*"I wish I were a dinosaur a-dozing in a*
>   *dingle,*
>*Or squelching through the swamplands*
>   *where the muddy waters mingle;*
>*(The dinosaur is noted for his very little*
>   *brain,*
>*But he has a lovely figure, like an*
>   *indiarubber train.)"*

Toby:

>*"I wish I were an octopus down in the*
>   *briny seas,*
>*With lots and lots of wavy legs and*
>   *suckers on my knees,*
>*And when I met another octopus, it*
>   *would be grand*
>*To shake his hand and hand and hand*
>   *and hand and hand and hand."*

Camellia:

> *"I wish I were a specimen of homo*
> *sapiens,*
> *Pursuing with intelligence my well-*
> *considered ends,*
> *A pentadactyl plantigrade, and rational*
> *as well —*
> *To be a homo sapiens, oh wouldn't that*
> *be swell!"*

"Oh!" said Toby at this. "I know that homo sapiens means people, but what's a penty-what-you-said?"

"A pentadactyl plantigrade," explained Camellia graciously, "is a creature with five toes, that walks on the soles of its feet. Like you. Now *I'm* an even-toed ungulate, which is much more useful in this sort of country. In other words, I've got hooves."

Just then it started to snow.

"Bother!" said Camellia. "This is going to make the sand all squelchy, and I don't think it is good for the cactus either."

"At least it's better than fog," said Toby. He sat huddled up on the camel's back, remembering that he had had no breakfast that morning. As the sun rose higher in the sky, however, he began to think that snow in the desert was not such a bad idea after all. At least it saved them

from getting too hot and thirsty.

Eventually the snowflakes began to stick to the ground, and to the camel's coat, and he scraped together enough to make a nice big snowball. As he sat up straight to throw it, the snow stopped as suddenly as it had begun. He could see a patch of purple moorland, and beyond it, something vast and flat and blue glittering in the sunshine.

"Whee!" he shouted. "It's the sea!" He hurled the snowball as far as he could, and started bouncing up and down in delight.

"Kindly desist from excessive bodily mobility," said Camellia. "In other words, do sit still!"

"But it's the sea, the sea, I see the sea!" shouted Toby. Hardly Visible suddenly piped up,

"A lady called Sheila C. Shaw
Saw a seesaw upon the seashore;
She saw more than I see,
For I can't see the sea,
Or the seashore seesaw She Shaw saw."

"Of course, I can see it really," he added, climbing up the camel's neck to get a better look. "Well done, Camelus Humpicus – even if you *were* looking for the river!"

"Hrrrmmmph!" said Camellia, which was her usual remark when she didn't know what else to say. They went on to the edge of the desert, and across the patch of moorland with its heather and little scrubby bushes, and found themselves on the top of a cliff, overlooking a wide bay.

49

There were no houses in sight, but a well-worn path led along the cliff top.

"Left or right?" asked Camellia.

"Right," said Toby.

"Left," said Hardly Visible.

"Right it is, then," said Camellia, and they set off in that direction.

6   Fiddlington-on-Sea

Toby, who was tired of sitting on the camel's back, got down and walked beside her. They could hear the waves breaking on the beach below, and overhead a few seagulls were soaring on the wind and giving excited cries. They passed a large crab, which had evidently found its way up from the beach.

"Excuse me!" Toby said to it. "We are looking for Fiddlington-on-Sea . . ."

"Never heard of it!" said the crab in a snappish fashion, and turned its back on them.

"Well, he's not very polite, I must say!" said Toby.

"Unconvivial behaviour typical of crustaceans," said Camellia. "In other words, crabby."

They trudged on until they got round the next headland, and suddenly they saw, spread out beneath them, a small town with a pier and a lighthouse. A steep, winding path led down from the cliff, and Camellia had to pick her way carefully, as it was not really meant for camels. They got down safely, however, and found themselves in a bustling little town with banners and bunting everywhere, proclaiming that Fiddlington Festival was now in progress.

Everyone was much too busy to take any notice of a small boy and a camel, but one man did look up from practising a bassoon in his shop doorway to ask if there was a circus coming. When they told him they were looking for a musical musing man who never spoke, he said,

"Ar, 'e lives in the last 'ouse down thrr. Roit boi the zee."

They found the house with its neat garden surrounded by a low stone wall, and a sign on the gate which read:

A. MUSER, COMPOSER
(Fried fish a speciality).

"It would appear more expedient for me to remain in the less immediate vicinity," said Camellia. "In other words, I'll stay here." She did not, in fact, have much choice in the matter, as she would never have fitted through the tiny garden gate.

Toby went up the path and rang the bell.

Before the silvery chimes had died away, the door was opened by a short, dumpy man with a bald head and steel-rimmed spectacles, who was wearing full evening dress. Toby thought it was best to come straight to the point.

"I've come about a tuning fork," he said. He had expected Mr Muser to make signs in reply, so he was quite startled when he sang out in a deep, booming voice, to the tune of the chimes of Big Ben,

"Well, well, well, well!
Do come in, please!"

He led Toby into a cosy sitting room, with polished oak furniture, and lots of gleaming brasses everywhere. A dumpy woman with a round face rather like her husband's came out of the kitchen to meet them. Through the open kitchen door there floated the sound of sizzling, and a delicious smell of fish and chips. Mr Muser sang out,

"Here is a boy who wants to buy
A tuning fork, I don't know why."

"No, I..." began Toby, but Mrs Muser butted in, to the same "Ding dong" tune,

"Welcome, welcome! Just wait two
ticks —
You're just in time for fish and chips."

"Oh, that would be great!" said Toby. Mr Muser waved an arm for him to take one of the big armchairs by the fireplace, and sat in the other himself, Mrs Muser disappeared back into the kitchen. A large, grey cat was sitting on the rug, and as soon as Toby sat down, it jumped onto his knee and started purring loudly.

"Hello, cat," said Toby. "Do you speak English? Most of the animals around here seem to."

"He does not speak," ding-donged
  Mr Muser,
"He only sings."

Whereupon the cat started a most dreadful "Yeeeeoooowl, Yeeeear-oooo-ooool!" until Toby couldn't stand it any longer, and put his hands over his ears. Mr Muser took the cat and chased it out of the house. When he came back, Toby said,

"From what I'd heard I didn't expect you to talk at all. Even singing, I mean. But at least you and Mrs Muser don't fight, do you?"

"Of course we fight!" sang Mr Muser.
"Both day and night!" echoed his wife from the kitchen.

Then she came out and asked if Toby would like to hear their quarrelling song. He was rather surprised at this, but said, "Yes please," politely, and the Musers started singing. This time the tune was "Pop goes the Weasel":

Mr M: *"Yes it is, I know I'm right!"*
Mrs M: *"No it's not, you're wrong, dear!"*
Mr M: *"Yes it is, it is, IT IS!"*
Mrs M: *"Don't interrupt, dear!"*

They stopped and both beamed at Toby.

"What a good fight!" ding-donged Mr Muser.
"Exactly right!" agreed his wife.

Then she told them to come into the kitchen, as the meal was ready. Toby found the kitchen table laden with plates of bread and butter, chocolate cake, cherry cake, ginger cake, fruit cake, cream buns, rock buns, doughnuts and coconut macaroons, not to mention a large teapot and milk and sugar. Mrs Muser went to the stove and served up three large plates of fish and chips with mushy peas, and they sat down to eat.

"Oh, I forgot," sang Mrs Muser.
"No knives and forks."

She went to the kitchen drawer and got out an ordinary knife and fork for Toby, a knife and tuning fork for herself, and finally put beside her husband's plate a tuning fork that made Toby gasp and open his eyes very wide. It was shining and gleaming with the most extraordinary colour he had ever seen. For a moment he couldn't think what it reminded him of, and then it came to him — it was *exactly* the colour of a skylark's song on a summer morning. It couldn't possibly be anything but the Great Glimrod!

7　The Great Glimrod

As soon as he got his breath back, Toby started to ask about Glimrod, but Mrs Muser told him to eat up his fish and chips before they got cold. For a while there was complete silence, because although it is possible (though not very polite) to speak with your mouth full, it is much more difficult to sing with your mouth full. Although Glimrod was quite a bit bigger than an ordinary tuning fork, Mr Muser didn't let that worry him, and shovelled in his fish and chips at a great rate.

When they had all had enough to eat (and a bit more besides), Toby thanked them for the meal. He was again going to ask about Glimrod, when Mr Muser suddenly got up from the table and started dancing around, waving it in his hand and singing (the tune was "Pop goes the Weasel" again):

"What a lovely tuning fork
To eat a pretty fish-wish!
Fish and chips and tuning fork,
Shimply de-lish-wish!"

With that, he danced out of the kitchen, through the sitting room, and up the bedroom stairs.

"Oh dear, oh dear!" sang Mrs Muser. *"He's drunk again!"*

"It must be that tuning fork he was eating with," said Toby. "Where did you get it?"

Mrs Muser explained (with much ding-donging and pop-goes-the-weasel-ing) that her husband's own tuning fork had got cracked, and he was just about to get it mended when he had had a great stroke of luck. They had had a great storm yesterday, and as soon as it stopped he had gone out fishing as usual, and had fished this beautiful new tuning fork out of the sea. Naturally, he had been delighted with it, but as soon as he had eaten his lunch with it he had been acting drunk for the rest of the day.

Then, at last, Toby got a chance to tell his own story. Mrs Muser said that of course Glimrod must be restored to its rightful owner at once, and she hurried off upstairs to tell her husband about it. Toby could not catch her words, but suddenly he heard Mr Muser's voice booming out,

"No, no, no, no!
No, no, no, no!"

Then a door was slammed loudly.

Mrs Muser came back, looking very upset, and explained that her husband had flatly refused to part with his nice new tuning fork, and what's more, had locked himself in the bedroom.

"Oh dear!" sighed Toby. "Whatever can we do now?"

"If I may make a suggestion," said a bump on the carpet suddenly. Mrs Muser nearly jumped out of her skin.

"It's all right," said Toby. "It's just a chameleon friend of mine."

"Why don't we take the cracked tuning fork ourselves and get it mended?" asked Hardly Visible. "Then perhaps Mr Muser will be willing to exchange it for the Glimrod fork when he is sober."

They agreed that this was an excellent idea, and Mrs Muser got the cracked tuning fork for Toby, and came to the door to see them on their way. It was now raining heavily, and Camellia was still waiting by the front gate, looking very damp and miserable.

"Am I justified in surmising a satisfactory outcome?" she asked. "In other words, is that it? It just looks like any old tuning fork to me."

"I'll explain on the way," said Toby, and he turned to wave goodbye to Mrs Muser with the cracked tuning fork. "I'm glad we have found Glimrod anyway," he called out to her. "We'll soon get things put right again now."

They set off again up the main street of the little town. Meanwhile, the Musers' cat, who was still outside, chose that moment to jump onto the back garden wall. He saw crouching behind it a dreadful cat-like creature ten times bigger than himself, and a large, green crocodile. He let out a bloodcurdling howl, and ran back into the house. Unfortunately, however, the noise was so much like his normal singing voice that no one took any notice.

8 Kipper Capers

Slubblejum was delighted to have discovered – as he thought – the mysterious object they were looking for.

"So *that's* the Great Glimrod," he said, half to himself and half to Ug. "It's not much to look at, but they do say all that glitters is not gold, nor iron bars a cage. Now all I have to do is lay a little ambush." He decided that the slow-moving crocodile would only get in the way.

"Stay here!" he hissed at it. "*Sit*, understand?" Don't move till I get back." Then he raced off up the back street of the little town, and along the cliff path until he found a stunted old tree, its branches all twisted by the wind from the sea. He quickly climbed it, and settled down to wait until Toby and the camel would pass underneath. Then he would grab Glimrod and become Slubblejum the Great, King of the Wind and the World.

Meanwhile, unfortunately for him, Toby and Camellia had stopped to ask a village lady where they could find a blacksmith's shop. After the fashion of people in those parts, instead of giving a straight answer, she had said,

"Want some new shoes for your camel, do you, dearie? Well, now, I never knew as camels wore shoes like 'orses." Toby explained that they were just doing a favour for Mr Muser, and the lady had proceeded to hold a long conversation about her odd neighbours and the funny weather they had been having recently, before finally telling them they would have to go to the next village to find a blacksmith.

By this time Ug, who was not the most obedient of crocodiles, had got bored with waiting behind the Musers' house, and had made his way up the hill. He waddled out from behind a bush just as Camellia, with Toby once more on her back, was setting off along the cliff path. Camellia took one look at the crocodile, shied like a frightened horse, and bolted — straight for the edge of the cliff.

"STOP!" shouted Toby, but it was too late. Camellia braked very suddenly with a screeching of hooves, and stopped dead. Toby, still clutching the cracked tuning fork, shot into the air over her neck. He flew out over the cliff in a big, graceful arc, and then went head over heels down into the sea, where fortunately it was now high tide. He felt himself sink through the waves for what seemed a very long time, then finally landed on the seabed with a bump.

When he got his breath back, he realised he would have to swim to the surface to see which way the shore was. But as soon as he set off swimming, he found he was being swept along by a strong current. It was simply impossible to fight his way up to the surface, and at last he gave up and let himself sink down to the seabed again. He sat down on a rock with his head between his hands, feeling very discouraged.

He gradually became aware of a strange noise all round him, like a kind of whispering and giggling, as if a crowd of small children were trying unsuccessfully to keep quiet. He lifted his head and looked round, to find that he was sitting in the midst of a shoal of orange-coloured fishes.

"Why, who are you?" he asked in surprise.

"We're kippers, of course."

"Giddy kippers."

"The kippers of Kippernia."

"Fancy not knowing a kipper when you see one!"

The chorus of answers came from all sides at once.

"But I thought kippers were sm..." Toby was going to say "smoked", but he suddenly thought they might be offended, so he said,

"smaller than you" instead, which didn't make much sense.

"Oh, no, we're the small ones."
"We are only young kippers."
"We're on our way to school."
"We are the kipper nippers."
    came the chorus.

Then one of them started singing, and the rest joined in, while they all swam round Toby in big circles:

"It's great to be a kipper
At the bottom of the sea —
We do exactly what we like,
Then have a break for tea.

We chase the wild seahorses
And catch them with lassoes,

Or hunt the dreaded tiger fish
To put in oozy zoos.

We hold a kipper carnival
And climb the greasy pole,
We dance the kipparumba
And the kipparock 'n roll.

We play at kipper football
Down in the football pools,
And all the little kippers
Go to kipprehensive schools.

So kippers, flap your flippers,
And shout, 'Oh Kipperee!'
To be a jolly kipper
Is the only life for me!"

Then one of the kippers asked, "And what about you? What kind of animal are you? What funny fins you've got."

"Shhhh!" said another. "That's not polite."

"Well, why should I be polite to a land monster?" demanded the first. "That's what you are, aren't you?"

"I'm a boy, as it happens," said Toby with dignity.

"I don't believe it," said another. "There's no such thing as Boys."

"Of course there are," said yet another. "And he's one, so that proves it." With that, a great argument broke out among the kippers, until one of them shouted "Quiet!" at the top of his shrill, piping voice.

"Quiet!" echoed another, helpfully. "George wants to speak."

"The only way to settle the matter," said the one called George, "is to ask Mr Flounder. He'll know whether it's a Boy or not."

"Who's Mr Flounder?" asked Toby.

"He's the schoolmaster," said George, "and we're late for school already."

Toby didn't think much of going to school during the holidays, but he decided that perhaps this Mr Flounder might be able to tell him how

to get back to dry land. So he swam along with the kippers until they came to a clump of rocks, where the teacher was waiting for them, sitting in a floppy, floundery fashion on top of the largest rock.

"Oh yes," he said vaguely when Toby was presented to him. "A very fine specimen. Very clever of you to have caught it. Hmmmm, yes indeed!"

"But is it a *Boy*?" insisted George.

"Roll call!" shouted Mr Flounder, and he got out a large register from behind the rock. "We're fifteen minutes late already." Then he started reeling off names, while some of the kippers flopped onto the rocks, and others went on swimming round in circles.

"Arthur, Beatrice, Caroline, Daniel, Elvira, Francis, Gerald, Harriet," called Mr Flounder. He never looked up, or noticed that it was the same two or three kippers who were answering "Yes" to all the names.

"We take it in turns to answer," whispered George. "It makes life much simpler." Who for? wondered Toby.

"Ivor, Jacob, Katerina, Lewis, Mirabelle, Norbert, Oswald, Prunella, Quincey and Queenie…"

"Twins," whispered George.

"Robert, Stanton, Tessa, Ubald, Victor, Winifred, Xerxes, Yasmin, Zylaphina, Angela, Benedict, Coriolanus..."

Toby was wondering how long this would go on, but at this point Mr Flounder suddenly said,

"No more time today. I'll call the rest tomorrow. Now, today's lesson is Poetry. You there," he said, pointing a flipper at Toby, "It's your turn to read."

"But I'm only visiting!" protested Toby.

"Precisely!" said the flounder. "Take out your book."

Toby didn't know where to look for a book as there were no desks, but George produced one from behind a clump of seaweed and handed it to him.

"Please read the poem on page 234," ordered Mr Flounder, and Toby did as he was told. The poem certainly *looked* rather odd, but when he read it aloud it sounded quite normal. It went like this:

"The leaves are falling from the bough,
The wind is loud and rough,
When Farmer Brown goes off to plough –
He's burly, big and tough.

No shadow clouds his manly brough,
And yet his voice is grough,
Because he's caught a cold somehough
From taking too much snough.

He sees the piglets with their sough,
The chicks like balls of flough;
He hears the cat cry out, 'Meough!'
The dog replies, 'Wough, wough!'

He passes Buttercup, the cough,
And coughs behind his cough;
But that is quite enough for nough —
I never heard such stough!"

Mr Flounder made no comment on the reading, but took out a large whistle, blew it, and promptly fell asleep.

9 The Coral Palace

"School's over," announced George.

"That was a short lesson!" said Toby in surprise.

"What do you expect?" asked another kipper.

"We have two hours playtime..."

"...then twenty minutes break for lessons..."

"...then it's playtime again..."

"...for the rest of the day," said various voices.

"What are we going to do with the Boy?" asked George.

"It's not a Boy," said someone.

"It is a Boy," said George. "Mr Flounder said so."

"Didn't."

"Did."

"Didn't."

"Let's take him to the Queen," suggested a small, spotty kipper.

"The Queen!"

"Queen Kimmeranthia!"

"Off to the palace!"

"Don't forget to curtsey!"
came the chorus.

"There's a Grand Ball today because it's Tuesday," explained George.

"We have Sports on Monday..."

"Ball on Tuesday ...

"Seahorse races Wednesday..."

"Carnival Thursday..."

"Circus Friday..."

"Gala Saturday,"
said the shrill voices.

"Goodness!" said Toby, who was beginning to feel rather dizzy. "And what do you do on Sundays?"

"Oh, on Sundays," said George, "we have a holiday. Come on!"

Toby found himself being hustled along in the direction of a large pink and white mound he could see rising up from the seabed in the distance. As they got close, he saw that it had a large, arched entrance, above which was written

KIPPERNIA CORAL PALACE

As he followed George inside, his eyes were met by a scene of total confusion. They were in a great hall, its pink walls twinkling and shining as if lit up by hidden floodlights. A huge throng of kippers were dancing, or at least trying to dance, in the crowded space. Two separate bands were playing at floor level, and a third one up near the roof, not to mention one odd kipper who was wandering through the crowd playing a tin whistle.

A buffet was being served at the far end, and half the kippers were trying to get near the food, while the other half were dancing to various kinds of music, some doing a slow waltz, while the ones next to them were dancing a vigorous hornpipe.

Toby was led over to a large kipper who had a coral crown on her head, and a string of pearls round what might have been her neck, if you could tell where her neck ended and her waist began. All the young kippers bobbed up and down in what was obviously meant to be a curtsey, and Toby bowed very low. The Queen went on dancing on the spot as she asked,

"Well, and what have we here?"

"It's a Boy, Your Majesty," said George firmly.

"Isn't!" said a voice, and the argument broke out again.

"Silence!" roared the Queen above the noise of the dance bands.

"Well, *I* say he's a Boy," said George

stubbornly, "and I'd like to keep him please, Mama."

So George must be a prince, thought Toby. Fancy that! However, he found out later that the Queen had ninety-five children, and her eighty younger brothers and sisters had seven thousand, eight hundred and forty-two between them (at the last count). The Kippernians, in fact, were all so closely related that to be only a second cousin of the Queen was almost a disgrace.

"Well, if you wish, my dear," said the Queen, doing a little pirouette and heading off a passing balloon. "It would be just as well to keep an eye on him though, in case he's a spy." This caused a murmur of excitement among the young kippers.

"I'm afraid I can't stay very long, Your Majesty," said Toby. "You see, I'm really looking for a blacksmith . . ." Before he could explain, the Queen gave a roar of laughter.

"Dear me, you can't expect me to believe that!" she exclaimed. "You won't find a blacksmith in the sea, that's for sure. It would put their fire out, you know." And she started dancing a *pas de deux* with George.

"Yes, of course," said Toby, thinking how difficult it was to hold a conversation with someone who wouldn't keep still for one minute. "But you see, I wasn't looking for a blacksmith in the sea — that is, I got chased by a crocodile, and I fell off the camel's back and landed in the sea without meaning to."

The Queen thought this was even more funny, and bounced up and down with laughter, wiping the tears from her eyes. Eventually she said,

"You certainly have a good imagination, anyway. Riding on a camel and chased by a crocodile, that's a good one! You'll be telling me that cats have flippers next!"

"Well, not exactly," said Toby. "But the crocodile belongs to a nethercat — that's a kind of cat with scales like a fish, you know . . ." His voice trailed off as the Queen began roaring with laughter again.

"Dear me, you are a scream!" she said when she had recovered. "You can come and tell me some more stories tomorrow. I haven't had such good entertainment for months." With that she swam off, saying, "I must tell the Pilchard Ambassador — cats with flippers and camels riding crocodiles, haw, haw!"

After that, Toby was whizzed round from one dance band to the next by the crowd of young kippers, who did not seem to care much whether he was a spy or not. He enjoyed himself so much that he began to think maybe he would stay for a day or two after all. And by the time he had had a large supper, and settled down for the night on a cosy bed of seaweed, he had almost forgotten about the Lightning Conductor. And his time in the desert with Camellia just seemed like a distant dream.

I must see the races tomorrow, he thought. And then there's the carnival and the circus... and I wonder what they do get up to when they have a holiday on Sunday... Just as he dozed off, he decided there would be no harm in staying in Kippernia for a week — just to see all the events once round — and after that there would be plenty of time to think about blacksmiths and tuning forks and boring things like that...

10   At the Races

The next morning, Toby had a breakfast of
shrimps on toast, sprat flapjacks and sea cucum-
ber marmalade. It was not exactly what he was
used to, but it didn't taste too bad on the whole.
Then he was hustled off to school by the young
kippers, but when they arrived Mr Flounder
announced that today's lesson would be a project
on seahorses, so they all went off to watch the
preparations for the afternoon's races.

To Toby's surprise, the seahorses came in
every possible colour – red, green, blue, pink –
even some with spots or stripes on their backs.
George explained that they did not have riders,
but ran round the course by themselves, chasing
a small electric eel. He advised Toby to bet on a
handsome seahorse called Red Mud when the
bookies opened their stalls later.

Lots of other sea creatures were gathering

for the races, as well as the kippers. There were squids whizzing around like small torpedoes, lobsters and jellyfish, sea urchins and starfish, and Toby even noticed a dolphin swimming round the edge of the crowd and looking rather amused at the whole proceedings. He began to think he would like to be a marine biologist after all, instead of an entomologist. Suddenly, he heard a familiar squeak saying:

> *"There once was a large maharajah,*
> *Who went to a race with his charjah;*
> *He ran round the track*
> *With the horse on his back,*
> *For he was the one that was larjah."*

"Hardly Visible!" he exclaimed. "It's great to see you! I mean, not to see you," he added, looking all round, for the chameleon was even less visible than usual in the seawater. "I'm glad you didn't get lost at sea, anyway."

"Not at all," said the chameleon. "I've just been studying marine entomology – and very nice too!" He gave a jump onto Toby's arm, where he could be seen licking his lips.

"I'm just going to place my bet on Red Mud," said Toby, and then he remembered he had no money. He explained his problem to a passing kipper (who might have been George, or

then again he might not), and got the answer,
"Money – what's that?"

Then he saw that the kippers were handing
the bookies all kinds of strange objects as
bets – coral necklaces, cowrie shells, feather-
duster worms etc., and the bookies' stalls were
beginning to look more like a jumble sale than
anything else. He decided to risk his tea strainer
on Red Mud. The bookie – a large codfish – took
the strainer, removed a lollipop from his mouth,
said "Pick of the stall if you win," and went back
to sucking his lolly.

The racing was about to begin, and Toby made his way to the stand, which was a stretch of pink coral. The Queen passed by, wearing a large purple hat as big as herself, and nodded to him graciously.

"Ah, there's my little story-teller!" she said, and swept on towards the Royal Box.

When Toby reached the stand, he found himself next to Mr Flounder, who greeted him in his usual ponderous way, and asked him if he liked racing.

"Oh, yes Sir," said Toby.

"Harmless entertainment for the masses, of course," said Mr Flounder, "but some of us prefer more uplifting pursuits. Take poetry, for instance. I often write poetry myself, but alas, how rarely is it appreciated! As a matter of fact, I wrote a poem only yesterday – you wouldn't care to hear it, I suppose?"

"Oh yes, I'd love to," said Toby politely.

"It goes like this," said the flounder:

"The sky is blue, the grass is green,
The flowers are red, the grass is green,
The cows are brown, the grass is green –
The grass is green as green as green!"

"That's very nice," said Toby.
"Perhaps you would like to hear another one,"

said Mr Flounder, and without waiting for a reply he went on:

> *"Roses are red,*
> *Violets are pink,*
> *I'm feeling dead,*
> *It's time for a drink."*

"Yes, that's interesting," said Toby, "except that violets are not ... Oh well, never mind," he finished up, not wanting to hurt the flounder's feelings.

"How about this?" asked Mr Flounder:

> *"The sunflower's yellow, like the sun,*
> *The toad is spotted, like a bun;*
> *The toad is like a bun with spots,*
> *Among the blue forget-me-nots."*

"Charming!" said Toby.

"Glad you think so," said Mr Flounder modestly.

"But how is it that you write land poetry instead of sea poetry?" asked Toby.

"Oh, I love the land," replied the flounder. "Yes, indeed! It is so relaxing to go to the landside for a holiday, and watch that vast expanse of gleaming brown stretching away into the distance. But most of my poems are sad, I'm afraid," he continued with a sigh. "Take the one I wrote last week, for instance:

> *"This life is so full*
> *Of sadness and sorrow,*
> *Today is so dull —*
> *I wish it were next Saturday afternoon!*

"It makes me weep every time I think of it," he cried, taking out a large, spotted handkerchief.

"Yes, it is very sad," agreed Toby. "But I wonder, would it be even better, perhaps, if instead of 'next Saturday afternoon' you said, 'I wish it were tomorrow'?"

"Why, that's it!" exclaimed Mr Flounder, slapping Toby on the back with a large, wet fin.

You're an absolute genius! I wish I had a few more like you in my class — it would make teaching a pleasure, indeed it would!"

At this point, Toby felt something nudge his left foot, and as he looked down to see what it was, a small voice proclaimed in a stage whisper:

"There once was a very large flounder,
Who really was rather a bounder..."

"Hush!" interrupted Toby, giving the chameleon a poke with his foot. "That's hardly polite."

"That's Hardly impolite, you mean," retorted Hardly Visible. Then they all forgot about poetry as the first race began.

11   New Lamps for Old

When Slubblejum lost Toby and what he thought was the Great Glimrod in the sea, the first thing he did was to have a tantrum. Ug, who knew it was somehow all his fault, took one look at the mood the nethercat was in, and set off home as fast as his short legs would carry him.

"You no-good crocodile!" Slubblejum shouted after him. "You're as much use as a jelly hammer, you are!"

By next morning, however, the nethercat could look at things a bit more calmly. He did not know much about tuning forks, but he had heard of Aladdin and his wicked uncle, and it occurred to him that the shabby old tuning fork was pretty much like the shabby old magic lamp. All he had to do was to get hold of a nice new tuning fork, and persuade Toby to do a swap. He had a good idea where to find him – sooner or later he was sure to get mixed up with those crazy kippers who lived at the far end of the bay.

A couple of hours later, Slubblejum was back in the sea, and positively purring with satisfaction. He had picked a pocket or two among the crowds arriving for Fiddlington Festival, and had managed to provide himself not only with a brand new tuning fork, but also with a few other items like a mouth organ and a catapult which might tempt young Toby. He had then found a second-hand shop and bought an old raincoat and a sou'wester hat. With these on top of his scaly skin, he felt so well disguised that no one could possibly recognise him.

He arrived at Kippernia just as the first race was about to begin. And sure enough, there was Toby, conspicuous among the sea creatures, and talking to some fat old flounder. Everything was going according to plan.

Then suddenly the nethercat had a dreadful thought. Why hadn't he remembered it before? Of course, it was Aladdin's wife who had exchanged the old magic lamp for a new one, not Aladdin himself. Toby knew how valuable the old tuning fork was and he wouldn't be so silly – and he didn't have a wife to be silly for him, either.

But Slubblejum was not easily defeated, and he soon had a better idea. He started pushing his

way through the crowd behind Toby. The sea creatures cleared a way for him, as they did not like the look of the strange thing in a flapping raincoat, with a very unfishy face beneath its battered sou'wester.

There was a roar from the crowd as the first race began – the Novices' Handicap. The handicap consisted in the seahorses having to swim round the course backwards, and most of them found this so great a handicap that they got lost altogether, and swam off towards the open sea. This was the signal for hordes of excited young kippers to go and round them up. In the midst of all this movement and confusion, it was no problem at all for Slubblejum to slide a slippery paw into Toby's pocket, steal the cracked tuning fork, and leave the new one in its place. With any

luck, Toby would not even notice the difference until Slubblejum was far away and already King of the World.

When he got to the back of the crowd again, Slubblejum found he had just time for a flutter on the gee-gees before the next race – the Big Race – began. Feeling sure that this was his lucky day, he handed the mouth organ and the catapult to a codfish bookie who was sucking a lollipop, and placed his bet on Yellow Peril. Even as he did so, there was another great roar from the crowd, and the seahorses were off.

12   Life's Little Mysteries

Toby was delighted. Red Mud had come in first by a clear two lengths. He hurried off to collect his winnings. The codfish had said he could have the pick of the stall if he won, but unfortunately Red Mud was the favourite, and a lot of other people had got there first. Apart from which, he suspected that the cod bookie had hidden most of the best items for himself. By the time he arrived, there was not much left on the table but a handful of seashells and a small catapult, so he made the best of a bad job and took the catapult.

As he came away from the stall, he noticed that the dolphin he had seen earlier was giving rides to some of the younger kippers, with about twenty at a time on its back. How they managed to stay on, he couldn't imagine. He stood and watched while one load of kippers tumbled off at the end of their ride, and then, instead of picking up another load from the waiting queue, the dolphin swam away from them and stopped beside Toby.

"I do believe you are offering *me* a ride," said Toby. "That would be super!" The dolphin said nothing, but just smiled a knowing smile, and allowed him to climb onto its back. Toby grasped its big, black fin with both hands as it set off through the water at an amazing speed.

This is terrific! he thought. It's just like being on an underwater speedboat, and he's giving me a nice long ride as well. In fact, the racecourse and the crowd of spectators were soon out of sight, and as the ride went on and on, and got faster and faster, he became rather uneasy.

"Hey, dolphin, where are you taking me?" he called out. But the only answer he got was for the dolphin to make a great leap out of the water. Toby had just time to catch a glimpse of the shore before it dived in again, so smoothly that it hardly made a splash. He took a deep breath as they dived back into the sea, and found himself choking and spluttering. Something had gone wrong. They were back underwater again, and he felt as if he were drowning. He held his breath until his lungs felt like bursting and he thought he could hold on no longer.

Suddenly, he felt fresh air on his face again, and he found himself being put down gently but firmly on a sandy shore. He opened his eyes and saw the dolphin doing a sideways roll in the shallow water, as if to say goodbye, then it raced out to sea again, still smiling its mysterious smile.

Toby sat on the sand, feeling very shaky. Something climbed out of his pocket, shook the water off itself, and remarked:

"A fisherman wrecked in a gale
Rode back home on the tail of a whale;
When he told his dear wife
She exclaimed, "Pon my life —
That is really a whale of a tale!"'

"Oh, there you are, Hardly," said Toby.

"What do you think happened? I couldn't seem to breathe underwater any more."

"The effects of the super-duper tuning fork must have worn off," said Hardly. "It was bound to happen sooner or later."

"But how did that dolphin know it was going to happen just now?" asked Toby. "Well it's lucky for us that he did, anyway." Just then a familiar shape came plodding into sight at the far end of the beach.

"Camellia!" shouted Toby in delight. He scrambled to his feet and started running across the sand to meet her. Then he slowed down again, as he wondered what he was going to say to her. He suddenly felt ashamed of himself, because he had been enjoying a nice little holiday under the sea while she must have been worrying about him and looking for him everywhere.

Camellia saw Toby coming to meet her, and wondered what she was going to say to him. She felt rather ashamed of herself, because she had not stopped running away from the crocodile until she had got safely back to the desert. And had then felt so tired that she had slept all night and most of the next day when she should have been looking for Toby. As he caught up with her, she cleared her throat and muttered something about a "propitious renewal of our acquaintance." "In other words," she added, "I'm glad to see you again."

"Same here and likewise," said Toby. "I expect you've been looking for me everywhere, but all kinds of strange things have been happening since I saw you last." He told her about the kippers and the dolphin, and ended up, "Well, I suppose we'd better go and find that blacksmith, and get this old cracked thing mended." He took the tuning fork out of his pocket and looked at it.

"That's funny!" he said. "I can't find the crack." He inspected the tuning fork carefully, from every angle, then Camellia inspected it, and then Hardly Visible insisted on inspecting it, saying that his eyes were sharper than anyone else's. But whichever way they looked at it, not one of them could find the smallest sign of a crack in it. In fact, it seemed to be newer, brighter and shinier than it had ever been before.

There was obviously no need to find a blacksmith now, and Camellia said they were not far from Fiddlington, so they set off back to the Musers' house. Toby was in a thoughtful mood.

"I've never seen so many strange things in one day," he said. "But the tuning fork mending itself like that really beats the lot. It's quite

impossible, but it just happened."

"There are lots of strange things in life," said Camellia, and went on:

"Things to astound us are found all
    around us —
There's trees and there's bees and the
    odd U.F.O.
And the ten million bugs to be found in
    a jug
Of cold water (you ougther *say,*
cold H_2O)

Life is a wonder, no wonder we blunder,
For sages write pages but nobody
  knows —
We must develop a nose for the truth,
For a nose is a nose is a nose is a nose."

"Really, of course, love is the answer," she added as they went slowly on their way.

"What was the question?" piped up Hardly Visible.

"I've forgotten," said Camellia, "but it doesn't matter. Love is the answer, anyway."

They plodded on towards the Musers' house in silence.

13   Toby Gets the Wind Up

The three companions were once more in the middle of the desert, and Toby was annoyed about it. They had found Mr Muser quite sober, as his wife had managed to hide Glimrod that morning, and he had been delighted to get his old tuning fork back, especially when he heard it had been mended by magic. Apart from which, he had been too busy preparing for this evening's concert by the Fiddlington Philharmonic Orchestra (Conductor A. Muser, of course), to think about anything else.

So they were on their way with the real Glimrod at last. However, once they had got outside Fiddlington, an argument had arisen, because Toby was fed up of deserts, and wanted to follow the coast road until they came to the Catanooga, then follow the river upstream. But Camellia had thought they should keep well clear of rivers, because there might be too many nethercats and — er — other animals about. She did not mention crocodiles, but it was easy to see what she was thinking. They had asked Hardly Visible for his opinion, and he had said, in Camellia's best long-winded manner,

"Insoluble disputations may be determined by the arbitration of fortuitous randomimity. In other words, toss for it."

However, they didn't have a coin between them, and in the end Camellia had won because,

a) she was bigger, and

b) she had simply set off walking with everyone else on her back.

So now Toby had the sulks.

"I say!" remarked Hardly brightly. "Someone should write a poem about *us*. Camelli*a* and chamele*on*, you know." But neither Toby nor Camellia was in the mood for poetry, so he was quiet for a few minutes. Then he popped up again.

"Did you hear the one about the ostrich?" he asked.

> *"When asked why he buried his cranium,*
> *The ostrich said, 'Let me explainium —*
> *I feel simply grand*

With my head in the sand,
And I'm told that it's good for the
brainium.'"

After that, however, even Hardly Visible got tired of making conversation without getting any answers. The desert was behaving like a real desert this time, with no sign of fog or snow, and the sun was blazing down on them. Toby was getting hotter and hotter, and it was really the last straw when they saw the oasis in the distance, but Camellia refused to stop at it because she wanted to reach Halfway Hill before sunset. Then suddenly, he had an idea.

He knew it was a very bad idea, so he pushed it out of his mind. But the idea simply went out at one side, ran round the back of his head, and came in again at the other ear, so he had to listen to it. And the more he listened, the less it seemed like a bad idea, and the more it seemed like a good idea. And the more it seemed like a good idea, the more it seemed like a very good idea, until at last he could stand it no longer. He took the Great Glimrod out of his pocket, waved it in the air, and shouted at the top of his voice, as if he thought the finely-tuned instrument was very hard of hearing,

"O Wonderful Glimrod, send us a wind — send us a cool fresh wind from the sea!"

After that, everything seemed to happen at once. Camellia was so startled that she thought they were being attacked by a whole horde of crocodiles, and she started bolting across the sand at full gallop. Toby had to fling his arms round her neck and hold on for dear life. Almost at the same moment, he heard a great rushing noise behind them. The rushing grew to a roaring, and the roaring grew to a howling. And the howling grew to a great, spinning whirlwind that caught up with them, wrapped itself around them, plucked them up from the desert floor, and carried off into the air the boy, the camel and the

chameleon as if they had been a bundle of feathers.

Having started to gallop, Camellia didn't seem to know how to stop, so her legs went on galloping furiously, although her feet were no longer touching the ground. Toby soon felt giddy as they went round and round and up and up. All he could do was to close his eyes, cling to the camel's neck, and wish he had never left his uncle's farm. As for Hardly Visible, at the first sound of the whirlwind he had scuttled down inside Toby's shirt (which would have been very ticklish if Toby hadn't had something else to think about). And for once in his life he had absolutely nothing to say about anything.

How long this went on, none of them was very sure afterwards. Camellia said it was ten minutes; Toby thought it was more like an hour, while the thoroughly shaken chameleon declared it was at least three-quarters of a lifetime. But eventually the whirligig began to wear itself out. It went round in bigger and slower circles, and the air travellers could feel themselves gradually sinking back to the ground, until finally the whirlwind gave one last, tired, little sigh, and it was all over with a bump.

14   A Musical Interlude

After Toby and the camel had left, Mr Muser had a busy afternoon ahead of him. First, he had to print the programmes for the evening's concert. He got out the old duplicator, fed in some paper, and started turning the handle vigorously. After the first few copies, he stopped and checked that it was coming out right.

FIDDLINGTON PHILHARMONIC ORCHESTRA

Conductor – Amadeus Muser

GRAND FESTIVAL CONCERT

Beethoven	Fifth Symphony, in a new arrangement by A. Muser
A. Muser	Piano Concerto
	Soloist – Watchmi Ticklezekees

INTERVAL

A. Muser	Violin Concerto
	Soloist – Lotta Scratchenscrape
A. Muser	Seven's Company
	A diversion in 7/8 time for bassoon, tuba, double-bass, tom-tom, piccolo, vacuum cleaner and fire extinguisher

That looked correct, and he went on running off the copies, humming to himself as he worked. Then he saw that it was getting late. He had just time for a little snack of sardines on toast before dashing off to the Festival Hall for the concert, his suitcase full of the programmes. He found most of the players just getting out of an old double-decker bus with an open top, that belonged to the orchestra. It came in useful on occasions like this, as well as being used for concert tours.

The audience were gathering in quite large numbers, he was pleased to see, but the only problem was the weather. After snowing for most of the day, it had now decided that Fiddlington-on-Sea should really be on the equator after all. And the sun was blazing down so fiercely that the hall was becoming unbearable. After consulting with the manager, Mr Muser made an announcement that the concert would be held in the open air, and everyone trooped out onto the promenade in front of the hall.

The weather waited until everyone was settled, let Beethoven's Fifth Symphony begin – *Diddiddy-dum, diddiddy-dum* – then started pelting them with hailstones. Well, it was too late to stop now. Mr Muser went on conducting, the orchestra went on playing, and by the time they had got to the slow movement, the hailstorm had stopped and everything was going smoothly.

Then a camel fell on top of the kettledrums.

For a few minutes there was complete chaos. The members of the orchestra nearest the drums thought they were being attacked by Martians and ran for cover, knocking over the strings and the woodwind as they went. Some of

the audience scattered in all directions, while the braver ones stood their ground and started fighting with whoever was nearest.

In the midst of all this, Toby and Camellia sorted themselves out from the kettledrums, counted their arms and legs, and got rather shakily to their feet. Most of the audience had by now either run away altogether, or trooped back to the concert hall, threatening to lynch the manager if they did not get their money back at once. Mr Muser was still standing with his arms in the air and his mouth open, struck speechless, not to say songless. Then Mrs Muser, who had been sitting in the front row, gave him a shake

and pointed out who it was that had just fallen out of the sky.

Mrs Muser, in fact, seemed to be the only person who took the situation fairly calmly. First she picked up Glimrod, which had flown from Toby's hand and landed among the French horns. Then she told everyone to keep quiet and listen while Toby told them what had happened. When he had finished speaking, Mr Muser decided to turn pompous. He sang out, in his usual *ding-dong* tune,

> *"Dear me, dear me, what a to-do!*
> *We'll have to go instead of you.*
> *I'll never trust small boys again —*
> *This is a job for grown up men!"*

"What do you mean?" gasped Toby. "I know I made a mistake, but I won't do it again, I promise. We'll set off again straightaway, and take..." But Mr Muser wasn't listening. He had seized Glimrod from his wife, and was hustling her across the road and into the orchestra's bus. Most of the players who had not run away decided to pile in behind them. Mr Muser sang out an order to the driver, and before Toby really knew what was happening, the bus was off at full speed, and heading out of town.

"After them, Camellia!" he shouted. "It's *our*

job to hand over Glimrod, and I'm not going to let *them* do it!" He was trying to scramble onto the camel's back as he spoke, but of course he couldn't manage it, and had to wait until she knelt down on the ground. Then, as the bus struggled up the steep road that came out on top of the cliffs, Toby and Camellia set off in pursuit.

In the excitement, however, Mr Muser had forgotten that he did not have the faintest idea where they were going. So it was not long before the bus had to slow down and let Toby catch up, so that a rather shamefaced Mr Muser could ask him the way. They were now within sight of the Catanooga River. It was getting rather dark, and the bus driver suddenly decided they had gone far enough. There was no way he was going to risk driving the bus along a bumpy river bank in the dark, and besides, he'd already driven more than the maximum number of hours laid down by his union, and that was that.

There was nothing for it but to settle down to sleep in the bus. Mrs Muser, whose motto was, "Be prepared, the snack bars may be closed", had a pile of sandwiches in a carrier bag. Some of the orchestra had brought drinks and odd bars of chocolate with them, and they all had to be content with a small share each for their supper. All except Mr Muser, that is. He insisted it was not too late to catch a nice little fish in the river, which he cooked on a small camp fire before joining the rest of the party in the bus. He must have used the Great Glimrod to eat it, because he appeared rather unsteady on his feet as he got back into the bus. But he was not too drunk to keep a tight grip on Glimrod, and to remind Toby that tomorrow *he* would be the one to hand it over to the Lightning Conductor in person.

   "That way we'll make
   No more mishtakes," he sang. "G'night . . ."

15   Slubblejum Again

It was not long, of course, before everyone for miles around had heard that a small boy and a camel had flown through the air and landed at Fiddlington-on-Sea. And by the next morning, when the story reached Slubblejum, it had grown into a whole herd of flying camels, along with a cartload of kangaroos, and perhaps a giraffe or two.

Slubblejum was sitting on the river bank sulking when he heard the rumour. After discovering that the cracked tuning fork was no use at all for controlling the weather, he had been met by a furious Mrs Betaslink. For some reason she had refused to believe it was pure coincidence that the crocodile had wandered off by himself, and Slubblejum had suddenly been called to his aunt's funeral, on the very day they should both have been at the Croc of the Year

Show. But now Slubblejum started feeling much more cheerful. He realised that Toby must have the real Glimrod, and had been playing about with the weather. But that about the crowd of animals? If he had managed to collect some kind of bodyguard, Slubblejum would need help to deal with them. He decided to call a meeting.

An hour later, he had succeeded in gathering about twenty assorted nethercats, a few curious toads and water rats who watched from a safe distance, and a couple of duck-billed platypuses who were on holiday from Australia and looking for a bit of excitement. Slubblejum climbed onto a rock in the middle of the river, cleared his throat, and addressed the crowd.

"Friends, Romans, Nethercats, lend me your ears!"

"What did he say that for?" asked a small, purple nethercat who seemed to have an itch.

"It's in Shakespeare," said Slubblejum.

"But we're not Romans," said a long skinny-looking nethercat.

"Oh, do get on with it," said Mrs Betaslink. "I've got a lot of work to do."

Slubblejum tried again. "I have called you here to ask your assistance."

"What did he say about pigeons?" asked Granny Grizzleduff, who was as deaf as a post.

"I have called you here to ask your help," repeated Slubblejum. "I am sure you all know the

saying, 'A friend in need is better than no bread'."

"Yeeeeowp!" said somebody.

"Let me explain," said Slubblejum, raising a paw for silence. "You may or may not be aware that my rich Aunt Slipperminx has recently passed away and left me, among other things, twenty-six crates of tinned salmon."

A chorus of "Ooooo's" and "Ah's" greeted this statement, and the itchy one even forgot to scratch for a whole minute. Salmon did not live in the Catanooga River, and the only way the nethercats could get hold of such a luxury was by stealing it from humans, which was not easy to do. The idea of having twenty-six whole crates of it was beyond their wildest dreams.

"The salmon is hidden in a secret place known only to myself," went on Slubblejum. "And the tins can only be opened with a special key invented by my Aunt Slipperminx herself. You can therefore imagine my distress..."

"What kind of a dress?" asked Granny Grizzleduff, but no one took any notice.

"...my distress," went on Slubblejum, "when I discovered that this precious key has been stolen by a very unpleasant and cunning human child by the name of Toby. He has even had the cheek to leave a broken key in its place."

He held up the cracked tuning fork for everyone to see. None of the nethercats had ever seen such a thing before, but one of the platypuses remarked,

"We call that a tuning fork in Australia."

"Yes, that's right," said Slubblejum hastily. "We pronounce it tinning fork over here. Well, as I was saying, I have generously decided to offer a reward of a large tin of salmon to each and every nethercat who helps me to get back the stolen key. I am told that this Toby and a gang of his friends are at present making their way to Halfway Hill, where I intend to provide a little reception committee for them. Who will come with me? Will we let a gang of dastardly humans steal what rightly belongs to the nethercats?"

There was a chorus of such cries as "Nethercats for ever!" and "Death to the invaders!" and Slubblejum leaped down from the rock, feeling very pleased with himself for his eloquence.

"Follow me!" he cried, and set off at full speed out of the river, calling out all the slogans he could think of – "Once more into the breach, dear friends! Nothing succeeds like a silver lining! Climb every mountain! Leave no worm unturned! Keep right on to the end of the road..." Most of the crowd followed him, while Mrs Betaslink watched with her paws on her hips.

"Fiddlesticks and poppycock!" she said to anyone who was still there to listen. "If he has all that salmon, I'm a walrus! But I wonder what he is really up to, all the same."

She was right about the salmon, of course. Slubblejum hadn't got any, and wouldn't have given it away if he had. But he was sure that once he had the Great Glimrod between his paws, he would wield such power that no one would dare to insist on their reward anyway.

16   Disaster!

Toby and his companions woke early, feeling rather stiff and cramped from sleeping in the bus, on top of which Mr Muser had a hangover. Hardly Visible emerged from some corner or other and remarked,

> *"There was an old cockerel in Crewe,*
> *Who was partial to beer, the best brew;*
> *When daybreak was near*
> *He would sing loud and clear,*
> *'Cocka-hic-doodle, hic-doodle doo!'"*

There was not much for breakfast except some rather sour apples they picked from a nearby tree, and they were all glad to get on their way again. They set off following the course of the Catanooga upstream – the river bank was still wide enough to take the bus, though they thought they might have to abandon it later.

Mr Muser rode in the open top of the bus, saying that he needed fresh air, and still clutching Glimrod in his hand. Toby was offered a lift, but he preferred to follow behind on Camellia. He was still annoyed at not being trusted with Glimrod, and did not feel like talking to anyone.

The orchestra were in high spirits, however, in spite of everything, and as they did not have their instruments with them, they started to make music by singing some rousing choruses to help them on their way. Hardly Visible was also his usual cheerful self as he rode behind Toby on the camel.

"I say," he said suddenly, "would you like to hear the poem about the stubborn chameleon—

the one they recite to young chameleons to
teach them how to behave?"

"Not now, Hardly," said Toby irritably. "Tell
me later."

As the morning mist cleared, the sun had
come out again, and was once more threatening
to overdo it by making them too hot. Then, at
last, as they came round a bend in the river, they
saw Halfway Hill. But that was not the only thing
they saw, for there, waddling along the river
bank right next to them, was a large, green
crocodile. It was, of course, Ug, who had
managed to escape from Mrs Betaslink's back
cave, and was now following the scent of
Slubblejum and his companions.

At the sight of the crocodile, the bus driver came to a sudden halt, and Mr Muser gave a yelp and let Glimrod drop out of his hand, and straight into the crocodile's mouth. Poor Ug, who was already startled by the bus, suddenly found something hard and unpleasant in his mouth, tried to spit it out, and got it stuck fast between his teeth. Grunting and growling with anger, he scuttled away from the river bank, and across the fields towards Halfway Hill, hoping that Slubble-jum would remove the nasty thing for him. After a few moments of confusion, Toby persuaded Camellia to screw up all her courage and go after him, while the Musers and the orchestra scrambled out of the bus and started to follow on foot.

Slubblejum and his companions were just about to hide in some trees at the foot of the hill to wait for Toby, when the crocodile arrived. Slubblejum couldn't believe his eyes. Ug had brought him what looked like . . . yes, it could only be . . . the Great Glimrod!

"*Good boy!*" he exclaimed, as he prised it out of the croc's mouth. "I never knew you were such a clever crocodile, but they say dark horses run deep, don't they?" Then he saw Toby and Camellia coming in the distance, gave a great shout of "Victory!" and went bounding up the hill, his greeny-blue scales glittering in the sunlight. The rest of his party followed, with Toby and Camellia gaining on them fast. Then came the crowd of out-of-breath musicians, along with a couple of dozen small spectators in the shape of birds, rabbits, voles and suchlike, who had come to see what all the noise was about.

Slubblejum reached the top of the hill well ahead of everyone else, and turned to face his followers.

"Halt!" he cried, in a voice that could be heard a mile away. "Whoever comes one step closer will be struck by lightning!"

17   A Rainy Reign

When Slubblejum made his threat, one of the other nethercats called out,

"Stop fooling, Slubblejum. Where's our salmon?" The only answer he got was a flash of lightning that landed very near his feet. The nethercat jumped, and everyone else froze in their tracks. Toby and Camellia were now about halfway up the hill, with the orchestra behind them, while most of the nethercats had nearly reached the top, and formed a semi-circle in front of Slubblejum, who was silhouetted against the skyline.

Slubblejum shouted an order to Toby. "Dismount, human whelp! No one is to remain seated while King Nethercat is standing." Toby obeyed, and even at that distance he could see the grin of satisfaction that spread over Slubblejum's scaly face as the sense of power gripped

him.

"Salmon!" he cried. "Who cares about mere salmon! This, my friends, is no tin opener." He waved the strangely-coloured tuning fork wildly above his head, in case anyone had not yet seen it. "This is no less than the Great Glimrod, the power that controls the weather. And let me remind you that whoever controls the weather rules the world. Namely ME! Here begins the reign of King Slubblejum the Magnificent!"

"Hail, King Slubblejum!" shouted one of his old cronies, and some of the other nethercats decided to join the winning side, and started clapping and cheering. Slubblejum looked out over the Catanooga Valley, then slowly turned to the other direction, where they could see the golden desert shimmering in the distance.

"I decree," he shouted. "*We* decree," he corrected himself, "that henceforth, forthwith and heretofrom,"

"Hurray!" said one of the platypuses,

". . . that herewith, henceforward and hereinunder," went on Slubblejum, "all deserts will be abolished, as being too dry, too hot, and generally disagreeable."

This announcement was greeted by much cheering, back-slapping and paw-shaking among the group of nethercats, though no one else showed much enthusiasm, while Camellia was so shocked that she exclaimed,

"Execrable specimen of pisciform felinity! Who does he think he is?"

At that moment, however, there was a diversion, as someone came bounding up the hill from the direction of the river. Gleaming orange scales and a bright blue ribbon proclaimed it to be Mrs Betaslink, who was as usual very out of breath, and in a state of great indignation.

Ignoring Slubblejum's cry of "Halt!" she made straight for the crococile, who was just then creeping up on an unsuspecting fieldmouse, snapped a collar and lead round its neck, and then turned to shake her fist at Slubblejum.

"I knew you would be behind this, you young good-for-nothing!" she shouted. "And what are you doing up there, anyway? Playing I'm the King of the Castle, I suppose. Well, you ought to know better at your age. And the rest of you should know better than to encourage him," she added to the company of nethercats.

This insult to his new-found dignity was too much for Slubblejum. For a moment, Toby thought he was going to hurl Glimrod at Mrs Betaslink's head, then he remembered its power, and had a better idea.

"O Mighty Glimrod," he called, "I command you to take that interfering nether-woman out of my sight!"

Glimrod evidently knew who he meant, but it also seemed to be rather literal-minded, because a small, grey cloud at once appeared above Mrs Betaslink's head. It gently descended on top of her, so that she was wrapped in her own private patch of fog, and couldn't be seen at all. She could certainly be heard, however, as she ran round trying to escape from it, and shouting.

"Let me out of here!" and, "Wait, till I get hold of you, young Snatchington!"

Eventually she decided to grope her way back down to the river, with the fog following wherever she went. Slubblejum thought this was extremely funny, and began to really enjoy himself. He shouted at Glimrod again,

"Now, you old son of a firecracker, pour water on that desert, and plenty of it!"

The onlookers held their breath to see what would happen. All except Hardly Visible, that is. He chose that precise moment to say in a penetrating squeak,

"There once was a cat known as nether,
Who wanted a change in the weather..."

Toby hissed at him, "Hardly! This is not the time for poetry!"

"Hardly the time and hardly the place," said the irrepressible chameleon, "to show your hardly visible face."

Then even he was struck speechless as they saw what was happening. Although the sun remained shining above their heads, great grey clouds came racing across the sky, stopped when they reached the desert, and started pouring torrents of rain upon it. At the same time, there was a great roaring sound from the direction of the river. Everyone turned to see what it was, and saw rushing upstream a great wall of water. Toby had once seen the Severn Bore, and this was something like it, but much, much bigger.

The tidal wave hurled itself up the river with

the speed of an express train, and when it got opposite Halfway Hill, threw itself out of the Catanooga, and made a path for itself across the fields. It was like a completely new river flowing in the wrong direction. When it reached the desert, it poured itself out and was quickly swallowed up by the thirsty sand. The first tidal wave was followed by another, and yet another, so that even as they watched, the desert began turning into a vast, sandy swamp.

Slubblejum was delighted. He danced and cheered, then began turning somersaults on the top of the hill. He gave orders to Glimrod in quick succession. The watchers on the hillside found themselves first drenched with rain, then nearly blown off their feet by a howling wind, then nearly scorched as the blazing sun came out again.

While the desert became a swamp, Halfway Hill was rapidly turning into an island, as the tidal waves went on and on. Then there suddenly appeared over everything a beautiful rainbow. It was a magnificent rainbow, the biggest and brightest rainbow Toby had ever seen. There was only one thing wrong with it. It was upside-down. Its two ends pointed upwards like a vast cosmic grin on the face of the sky. It began to rock about above the clouds like a rowing boat on a stormy sea.

"Wowee!" said a voice near Toby. It was one of the duck-billed platypuses. "I've never seen anything like this in Australia!"

"Don't show your ignorance!" answered the other one. "It's because we are upside-down over here."

Toby had never felt so small and helpless in his life. Everything seemed to be turning into chaos, and there was nothing he could do but stand and watch. If only he could light a bonfire to summon the Lightning Conductor, but even that seemed impossible. He put his hands in his pockets, as if he hoped by some miracle to find a box of matches there. There were, of course, no matches, but there was one thing he had completely forgotten about in all the excitement — the catapult he had won at the races and that, if he had but known it, Slubblejum had lost.

It was no sooner thought than done. He took out the catapult, picked up a smooth, round stone from the hillside, then stood quite still and took very careful aim. At his first shot the stone flew towards the Great Glimrod as if it had been drawn by a magnet.

The Thunder-shaking
Lightning-waking
Hail and rain and rainbow-making
Snowflake-flaking
Earthquake-quaking
Wondrous Tuning Fork

flew out of the nethercat's grasp as if it had grown wings of its own, sailed up in a great arc through the air, right over the top of Halfway Hill, and away out of sight of the astonished Slubblejum and all the watchers on the hillside.

18   Out of the Blue

At the foot of Halfway Hill, on the southwest side, there was a small lake. On the lake there was a small rowing boat, and inside the rowing boat, still clutching the end of a large fishing net, although he was fast asleep, was a long, thin person, dressed in a grey top hat, morning coat and striped trousers...

The truth is that the poor Lightning Conductor had been working day and night for the past few days, and sleep had at last caught up with him. He was just having a pleasant dream about his last holiday on Ursa Minor, when he was woken by the splash of something falling into the water. He shook himself, wondered where he was for a minute, then pulled the fishing net out of the lake. There in the net, gleaming merrily the colour of nothing else on earth, was the Great Glimrod!

The Lightning Conductor was delighted. "I say, what a stroke of luck!" he exclaimed. "Found it myself after all. Now I suppose I'd better find that young Tobijones and tell him he can stop looking for it."

It was only then that he noticed that the small lake was rapidly turning into a large sea, and that something very odd was happening to the weather over Halfway Hill. He took one look at the upside-down rainbow, propelled the boat to the hill slope in about two seconds flat, and strode up Halfway Hill almost as fast as lightning itself.

"I think it's time to show oneself in one's true colours," he murmured as he reached the top of the hill and saw Slubblejum and the crowd gathered on the far side. He stood for a moment surveying the scene, and Toby and the others saw a tall figure that shone and glowed as if lit up by its own strange light. Its colour was not like that of Glimrod, but more like the colour of the calm after a storm, when everything is refreshed and wakes up to a new life.

All the animals and people went very quiet. Slubblejum shrank away from the Lightning Conductor, and Toby saw that the nethercat was shivering, as if he had suddenly gone very cold. Very quietly, the Lightning Conductor stretched out his right arm, pointing the skylark's-song-coloured tuning fork in the direction of the wet, swampy desert. He spoke in a very gentle voice, hardly more than a whisper, and yet somehow Toby could hear every word quite distinctly. He first spoke Glimrod's name, and then said to the tidal waves which were still hurling themselves onto the desert,

"Peace! Return to where you belong!"

Then he spoke to the dark, dancing clouds and the raging wind, saying,
"Hush! Be still!"
Finally, he addressed the strange, rocking rainbow,
"Right yourself, my friend, and be at rest!"
And the tidal waves turned round and began returning the stolen water to the sea. The clouds started scudding away and became white and friendly again. And finally the rainbow slowly turned itself in a great curve through the sky and came to rest between the distant hills. Everyone heaved a tremendous sigh of relief.

The Lightning Conductor let his arm drop and looked slowly round at the assembled company. Gradually, his colour faded into the familiar shade of blue, and his twinkling eyes came to rest on Toby, still standing with the catapult in his hand.

"Well done, my young friend!" he said.

Then he turned to Slubblejum, and neither of them said anything, but Slubblejum crouched to the ground and looked up at him with his tail between his legs, like a dog that has been caught stealing the Sunday dinner. The Lightning Conductor slowly began to smile.

"Funny thing about Glimrod," he said, patting it gently. "Perhaps I forgot to mention it. It's not so much *what* you say to it that counts, but how you say it. If you speak to it gently, you will get gentle weather, but if you roar like a hurricane, a hurricane is what you will get." He grinned down at the cowering Slubblejum.

"You haven't been standing on your head by any chance, old cat?" he enquired.

"Wrrrreeeeoooouuuuw!" said Slubblejum suddenly. He gave a great spring into the air, and set off with all the speed of his rippling, scaly muscles back to the river.

"I think you'd all better be getting along," said the Lightning Conductor to the company at large. "I'm afraid we have to finish the thunder-storm that was interrupted – mustn't disturb the balance of nature, what! But don't worry, friend camel," he added to Camellia, "it won't rain over your desert. Nothing but sunshine there for a long, long time."

Camellia said something that might have been "Hrrrmmmph!" or "Thank you," and set off plodding down the hill in the direction of the desert, which was already looking much more dry and dusty again. The nethercats set off slowly, then in bigger leaps and bounds, towards the river, followed by the crocodile with a trailing lead; the Musers and their orchestra waved a cheery goodbye and started heading towards their bus, while the smaller creatures began scuttling back to their nests and burrows and holes in the rocks.

"What about me?" asked Toby when they had nearly all gone.

"Well, what about you, old bean?" asked the Conductor.

"I mean, where shall I go?" asked Toby, rather bewildered.

"Why, home of course!" said the Lightning Conductor. "Cheerio, old fruit. I hope we meet again sometime."

Toby turned to go down the hill, and as he

did so, the air was split by a sudden flash of lightning, and almost at the same moment there was a tremendous roar of thunder and the rain began ...

He woke up to find his uncle bending over him.

"Are you all right, old man?" he was saying. "We were worried about you, out in this dreadful storm, but it seems to be stopping now. You've given yourself a nice bump on the head, haven't you? Never mind, I dare say you'll survive ..."

He went on, hardly giving Toby chance to get a word in, which was just as well, because he was too busy thinking about other things to talk. So it was all a dream, after all. He wondered for a moment if he still had the catapult, but it was gone. And so was the tea strainer, for that matter.

Ah well, he thought, if it was a dream, it was a jolly good one anway. I won't forget the Lightning Conductor in a hurry, or Camellia and Hardly Visible. And as for Slubblejum – I suppose anyone who can love a crocodile can't be all bad, after all. And he followed his uncle into the farm house for tea.

Epilogue

It was a few days after Toby's adventure in the thunderstorm, and nearly the end of his holiday. The bump on his head was already better and forgotten about, and he had just got a brand new insect net. He wandered down to the river to try it out, and sat on the bank for a while, listening to the gentle swishing of the water passing by. The weather was fine and settled, and he was nearly nodding off in the warm sunshine, when he *distinctly* heard a small voice reciting:

> *"There was a chameleon lived in a tree,*
> *And he thought he was clever as clever*
>   *could be —*
> *Hey, ho, sing me a song,*
> *Follow your nose and you'll never go*
>   *wrong!*

His mother had told him, 'Change colour,
* my son,'*
But he thought staying green would be
* much better fun —*
In autumn the leaves turned to red
* overnight,*
But he went shining on like a green
* traffic light.*

An eager old hawk saw him five miles
* away,*
And he said, 'I'll have greens for my
* dinner today!'*
He swooped like a dive-bomber down
* from the heights,*
And ate that chameleon up in two bites.

The moral's as clear as a fine summer's
* day —*
Just don't be conspicuous in any way.
So do what the crowd has decided upon,
(But only if you are a cha-me-le-on!)"

A movement caught Toby's eye, and he
thought he saw something scuttling away
through the long grass. But he couldn't be quite
sure because, after all, it was hardly visible . . .